William Ged, Edward Rowe Mores

Biographical Memoirs of William Ged

William Ged, Edward Rowe Mores

Biographical Memoirs of William Ged

ISBN/EAN: 9783337375560

Printed in Europe, USA, Canada, Australia, Japan

Cover: Foto ©Raphael Reischuk / pixelio.de

More available books at **www.hansebooks.com**

BIOGRAPHICAL

MEMOIRS

OF

WILLIAM GED;

INCLUDING

A PARTICULAR ACCOUNT

OF

HIS PROGRESS IN THE ART

OF

BLOCK-PRINTING.

LONDON,

PRINTED BY AND FOR J. NICHOLS,

MDCCLXXXI.

ADVERTISEMENT.

TO the fimple and unvarnifhed tale here laid before the Reader, no formal Introduction is neceffary. The Editor expects from it neither fame nor profit. The only fhadow of merit which he can claim is, the having refcued from oblivion fome authentic documents of an ingenious though unfuccefsful invention, and fome fugitive memoirs of the inventor and his family.

The firft part of the pamphlet is printed from a MS. dictated by the elder WILLIAM GED, fome little time before his death, for the fatisfaction of his relations. The fecond part was written by his daughter; to whofe benefit the profits of this publication (if any fhall arife) will faithfully be applied. The third part is lite-

rally

rally copied from fome Propofals publifhed by
JAMES GED in 1751, in a half fheet in 4to.
The Narrative of Mr. MORES is annexed, to
complete the fubject.

J. N.

July 12, 1781.

I. Mr.

I. Mr. WILLIAM GED'S NARRATIVE

SCHEME FOR BLOCK-PRINTING.

Dictated by himfelf fome time before his Death, for the Satisfaction of his Relations.

I HAPPENED in the year 1725 to be in company with a printer, who, talking of the lofs our nation was at for want of a letter-founder, and after fhowing me the nature of the types fingly and compofed in pages, afked me, if I could contrive a method to remedy that defect. I anfwered, That I judged it more practicable for me to make plates from the compofed pages than make fingle types. To which he replied, That if fuch a thing could be done, an eftate might be made by it. I defired he would give me a page for an experiment, which, after fome days trial, I found practicable, and fo continued for near two years improving on my invention; and making a great many experiments, feveral of which were expenfive; but the more I practifed, and the lefs chargeable materials I ufed, I was the more fuccefsful, till at laft I brought it to bear, as that no diftinction could be made between the impreffion from my plates and that from the types.

B -

I then

I then applied to a Gentleman in this place, who had five or fix thoufand pound ftock, and who for a fourth fhare of the profits contracted with me to advance all the money that might be neceffary for carrying on the work. But this Gentleman, afterwards converfing with a certain other printer in this town, was made to believe that £ 8000 would not bring that undertaking to perfection ; which did fo intimidate him, that in two years continuance of that contract, he made no farther advance to me than £ 22. So finding no appearance of fuccefs that way, I was glad of any opportunity by which I might expect better encouragement.

In July 1729, William Fenner, a London ftationer, being by accident here in Edinburgh, hearing of my project, made me propofals more difadvantageous than my former bargain, which however I accepted of. He claimed the half of the profits, in confideration he was to advance all the money requifite, and that I fhould procure my former partner's renounciation of any farther concern with me in that affair ; which being obtained, we entered into a contract for twenty-one years, by which I was obliged to communicate to him the art.

On his part he was obliged, four months after date, to have a proper houfe and all materials in readinefs at London, where I engaged to be by that time ; and thefe conditions under a penalty of £ 1000 to be forfeited by the party failing. There was likewife a claufe in that contract, that, if in eight months after trial, my project fhould not prove advantageous,

becaufe

becaufe of the oppofition it might likely meet with from the printers, in fuch event the contract was to be void and null.

I implemented my part by being at London within the time limited, where I found Mr. Fenner had no-thing agreed on provided, and I believe was as little capable. But being a ftranger to his circumftances, he made me believe, the reafon of this delay was, that he had got acquainted with a letter-founder, who would, for one 16th fhare from each of us, furnifh all the different types fhould be wanted; upon which followed another contract, and we were ac-cordingly furnifhed with two parcels of different types : but when we came to ufe them, we found them altogether unfit for our purpofe; and were like-wife informed, that he had been formerly employed by the King's printers, but was rejected by them, becaufe one Caflon had eclipfed him in his bufinefs, which occafioned his applying to me, believing he could make a living by the profits he expected from his fhare in my project. Thereafter having feen a Bible printed in the King's-houfe in London on a beautiful letter, I applied to them, to know if they would give fuitable encouragement to furnifh them with plates for a Bible from that type. Accordingly a day was appointed to hear our propofals : in the mean time they acquainted their new founder Caflon, who told them he would give us fifty guineas, if we, in half a year's time, made one page of a Bible from that type. Our appointment holding, we made de-mands, and they made offers of money, and we believed

we

we might have agreed ; but at the same time told us
of the above fifty guineas, and that the gentleman
who had made the offer was in the house; being called
into our company, he bragged much of his great skill
and knowledge in all the parts of mechanism, and
particularly vaunted, that he, and hundreds besides
himself, could make plates to as great perfection as
I could; which occasioned some heat in our conversa-
tion, and which was diverted by a proposal of Mr.
Basket, That Caslon and I should each of us have a
page given us, to make a plate from, of that type,
between then and that day se'nnight; and that he who
failed should give an handsome entertainment to the
company: this being agreed to, Mr. Thomas Gib,
overseer of the printing-house, was appointed judge
of the performance.

Next day, about dinner time, each of us had a page
sent us. I imeadiately after fell to work, and by
five o'th'clock that same afternoon I had finished
three plates from that page, and caused to take impressions from them on paper, which I and partners
carried directly to the King's printing-house, and showed them to said Mr. Gib, who would not believe
but these impressions were taken from the type;
whereupon I produced one of the plates, which, he
said, was the types soldered together, and sawed
thorough. To convince him of his mistake, I took
that plate from him, and broke it before his face,
then showed him another, which made him cry out,
He was surprized at my performance, and then
called us to a bottle of wine; when he purposed I

should

should take eleven pages more, to make up a form, that he would see how it might answer the sheet-way. My too expeditious performance here proved rather a detriment then advantage to me, as I came afterwards to understand from the King's printers themselves; who having acquainted Mr. Caslon with what had happened, he declined keeping the appointment in person, but sent a son of Mr. Basket's to tell, " That he could not perform the thing himself, nei- " ther could he get one of the hundred he spoke of " to undertake it."

Thomas James, the letter-founder above-mentioned, our partner, having a brother an architect, who was universally acquainted with the nobility and dignified clergy, he gave him one of these plates, and informed him of my above performance. Mr. James handed the plate about, till he came to the earl of Macclesfield, who told him, That there was a vacancy in the university of Cambridge, who would be glad to receive us, and let us have the privilege of printing Bibles and Prayer-books; which motion took. So John James the above architect, and my partner Fenner, went down to Cambridge, where their proposals were readily agreed to. But, before this time, I suspected much the sufficiency of my partner's circumstances, which made me tell, That I inclined to leave them at the term of the eight months; which John James hearing, being a man of substance, made an overture, to divide in four shares, and that he would make the fourth partner; that he would lay me down £ 100; that I should have

yearly

yearly £ 100 paid me for the ufe of my family, befides thirty fhillings weekly for my own fubfiftence;
that I fhould be præfes of the company; and that
any one of the other three partners, who joined voice
with me, fhould determine the queftion; and that,
laftly, he would ufe his intereft with the univerfity of
Cambridge, that I fhould have their privilege for
printing the before-mentioned books in my plate-way.
Which conditions I went into, and had the faid £ 100
laid me down.

We had feveral meetings at making up this contract; which being agreed to in the terms above,
was put into hands of counfellor Hamilton, to be
extended at large. Mean while the King's printers, having heard our defign, applied to the univerfity, and made an offer of £ 500 more than what they
had agreed to take from us. Afterwards Thomas
James, our letter-founder, fell to intriguing with the
King's printers (who underftanding the countenance
we were likely to obtain from the univerfity of Cambridge, which was equal to their own as to the privilege of printing Bibles and Prayer-Books; and the
more afraid, of having a man of fuch fubftance as
John James his brother partner with us) in order to
withdraw his brother, which afterwards appeared he
had undertaken to do. The argument they made ufe
of to fpirit him up (we having complained of the infufficiency of his types) was, to make him believe
that the fault lay in my plates only, and not in his
types, though they had been formerly rejected by
themfelves: wherefore, to convince his brother of
ignorance

ignorance or malice, I made impreffions from both type and plate, in the manner following; viz. Having at that time five or fix fheets of an octavo Prayer-book in plates made from the fame types, I caufed to make up a fheet, where pages of plate were inter-mixed with pages of type; and having twenty fuch fheets to caft off, I afked him, before his brother, to diftinguifh which was plate, and which type. To do which, he divided the one half of thefe fheets from the other, faying, the one was plate, and the other half type, whereas each of thefe fheets bore a mixture of pages, half one, half other. I made a fecond trial, on Thomas James's bringing two paragraphs of a dif-ferent fize of letter, compofed in Latin, which he de-fired to be caft off with care, being to be fent to the country for a fpecimen. Obferving this to be a bet-ter type than what he had furnifhed us, I caufed to make up as much of our letter as would make a folio-page, joined with thefe two fpecimens, from which I made a plate, and caufed to throw off a parcel of fheets from both, which being brought to him, he miftook the one for the other; but carried one of each home with him, and next day he difcovered a fmall open in the tail of one fingle letter, whereby he was afterwards capable to diftinguifh that plate from the type : for which reafon I made another plate from the fame compofed page, and caufed caft-off an equal number from the laft plate as from the former; and the impreffions being mixt and laid before him, he difcovered his ignorance, by affirm-ing that all the impreffions of my laft plate were

taken

taken from the types (not finding that chafm or open in a letter of the former plate), till I convinced him of his error by fhowing him the other plate. Not long after this, Mr. Samuel Palmer (the moft knowing printer in London), who had frequently feen my performance in the plate-way, affured me, that the types I was ufing were altogether unfit for my purpofe; and further, he and another gentleman told us, they heard our letter-founder fay, That as long as he was our letter-founder, we fhould never hurt the trade, and it was for that reafon he had joined us in company. Having wrought about eighteen months at London on feveral books with thefe imperfect types, which proved naught, and the leafe never yet obtained, though the univerfity fent letters every two or three weeks to John James our partner at Greenwich, directed to the care of his brother the letter-founder at London, who, being in ufe of breaking-open thefe letters, kept up a material one, wherein the univerfity defired us to take counfel, and talk with their agent at London, to whom they had fent their papers and powers. Next meeting, inftead of communicating the contents of this letter to the concerned, he told them, He had feen a gentleman, who faid the gentlemen of the univerfity were furprized we had fo long delayed coming down to Cambridge to take out our leafe, which they were fo willing to grant us, and propofed to his brother and Mr. Fenner to go down in name of the company, which they had agreed to before I came. When they told me what had paffed, I, know-

ing

ing the man's fincerity, which I had obferved for fome time before, thought it not convenient without I went along with him ; and then told them, I could endeavour to procure the recommendation of my Lord Iflay and others of my countrymen : and accordingly I obtained my Lord Iflay's letter to Mr. Smith, profeffor of the opticks in Trinity College, who happened to be præfes at that meeting, called Syndicks. This letter I delivered by myfelf, when this gentleman afked me what advice I had from counfel about their privileges ; which was the firft time I had heard any thing of the contents of the above-mentioned letter from the univerfity. This being a farther confirmation of this man's treachery, I let Mr. Smith know my former jealoufies of him ; and, fince he was præfes, I begged of him to call a meeting before I left this place, that I might know their opinions ; and accordingly being met, they granted our requeft for paying into the univerfiry £ 100 yearly, and five pounds *per annum* to one Jonathan Plinder, an old decayed printer in that place. I told Thomas James, I was informed fuch a letter was fent by the univerfity to his brother, to take advice of counfel as it directed, and was much furprized he had concealed the contents from the company ; when he anfwered, he did not know the ufe of it. I defired him to go along with me to thank the gentlemen of the univerfity, which he refufing, I told him I would go alone then ; but feeing me pofitive, we went in company ; when he, with no little affurance, afked them, That if my project

C   fhould

should misgive, were we obliged to pay them an hundred guineas yearly? and farther he doubted of the validity of their lease. To both which they answered, We had to do with gentlemen; and then we got their decree signed unanimously. When we came to London, I acquainted my other partners with my success at Cambridge, and Thomas James's behaviour and concealment of the forementioned letter. His brother took him heartily to task; who told me how he had chastised him, and got his promise of better behaviour for the future. Then we resolved to go all together to Cambridge, to attend two other courts, called Caput and Convocation, to get the finishing stroke to their lease. We appointed a day to set out; but Thomas James thought fit to inform the King's printers (our antagonists) of our resolutions, who had been at Cambridge two days before we arrived, and had renewed their former offer of £500 to the university, besides an yearly premium; and the more to ingratiate themselves, carried along with them specimens of Caslon's types, to shew the imperfection of Thomas James's, as were exhibited before himself, when he was obliged to own there was no comparison: but, having an impression of that plate with me I had formerly made from Mr. Caslon's types, made it plain, my work must be always answerable; which the gentlemen being convinced of, our lease passed the other two courts next day. The university being confined to make that grant only in the name of one single person, we were asked which of us should be nominated; when Fenner and

Thomas

Thomas James ftood candidates, and, by the power
given me of the cafting vote, I gave it in favour of
Fenner, who. promifed, as foon as he came to London, to make a transference to the whole concerned;
but no fooner we returned thither, than there was a
propofal made to fend Thomas James to Holland
to purchafe proper types, which was accordingly
done, when in two months ftay there, he brought upon
us a charge of £ 160, and only one fet of types home
with him, though in greater quantity then he had
either orders or we ufe for. Having heard me frequently fay, that the beft plates I could make would
be from types before they were ufed or inked, he
caufed to fet up four pages of a Bible, to make a plate
from them, before any impreffion had been taken
from them. The impreffions were made, when there
appeared like two hundred blots in each page, which
he was fo fond of, that he carried them directly to his
brother. Being furprized, I caufed take impreffions
likewife from the types, when the fame number of
blots appeared there too : and when the compofitors
obferved the types, they told me, that about a third
of them had never been adjufted ; then James himfelf was fet to adjuft them. After this, I made a
whole fheet of a Bible, and impreffions were taken
from both type and plate ; when Thomas James
brought a quire of fine paper, and was prefent at the
impreffion taken from the type, and placed his feal
on the middle of each fheet. Seeing his eagernefs
to catch advantages, I went for a quire of the fame
kind of paper, and defired him to be witnefs to the

impreffion

impreffion from my plates; and having ftamped my feal likewife on each fheet of mine, both impreffions were fhewn to Samuel Palmer and his brother, who were fatisfied with the performance. This was fomewhat grating to Thomas James. The next malicious ftratagem he fell upon (being witnefs to the taking of thefe impreffions) was, to acquaint his brother with the defect of the impreffions in the corner of one of the fheets, which he had picked out on purpofe, which defect was owing to the platten's being patched with paper; but as his was firft caft off, there were more of them injured in that particular place than of mine; which fhewing his brother, and convincing him of his malice to the undertaking, he confented that he fhould have no farther concern, or be allowed to come to our meetings, which occafioned the delay of our contract, and confequently of the transference, not knowing whether he was to be any more a partner. Then we got compofitors, and fet to work about a Bible and two Prayer-books on that letter brought from Holland; two Prayer-books upon a Brevier letter, which we had from Thomas James, which were laid afide after four fheets were made in plates; and likewife an octavo Prayer-book, whereof nine fheets were made, and likewife thrown afide, which afterwards, when I left them, they completed in the common way. I made likewife plates for a Grammar, when my partners made choice of an overfeer, who did not underftand the rudiments. At this time we had about a dozen compofitors, and finifhed two Prayer-books, without

taking

taking an impreſſion of one ſheet; being obliged to make two plates for each page (and very often a greater number, till he was ſatisfied that he had got two ſufficient for the work): this learned overſeer was made judge, to break down what he thought convenient to be caſt over again; but his judgement ſhewed itſelf in breaking the beſt, which I frequently diſcovered, and ſhewed him the plates after broke, to give him reaſon to be convinced of his error; though all the excuſe he made for himſelf was, that there were faults in the compoſing, which ſhould have been his buſineſs to have known before they were brought to me. Having obſerved this practice ſo frequently, I made my complaint to Mr. Fenner, that impreſſions might be taken of the whole work, to ſee how far we had been impoſed on: Fenner not ſeeming to agree to it, ſurprized me much, my demand being ſo juſt. A little after I came to diſcover, that there was an underſtanding between Fenner and this overſeer, who was likewiſe clerk to the diſburſements, of which John James bore the far greater ſhare, without ever taking receipts or clearing accompts with Fenner, who had his game to play with this clerk in making up the accompts; as he told me afterwards, that he had a promiſe of fifty pounds from Fenner, to make up the accompts as he ſhould direct, and to continue him in his favour; and he added, that it was then in his power to diſcover to me, how far Fenner deſigned to trick and play the rogue both againſt John James and me. But having in due acquainted Mr. James with my obſervations

and

and fufpicions of this overfeer, we determined to employ a more proper man, to whom we would allow
double the wages that the other had. Accordingly
another was got, who feeing the former's performance,
and efpecially that on the Grammar, he let us fee, there
was like twenty errors in every page, and all the
reft of his work fhewed he had no judgement in the
matter. Our new overfeer immediately propofed to
get Dutch preffmen, and we immediately fent him
to Holland to fetch them over; and in the mean
time our old overfeer was continued till the other's return, and, knowing he was to be no longer employed,
he committed rather greater blunders than formerly:
but before our new overfeer went away, being acquainted with the King's printers, informed them of
the advantageous offers we had made him, and his
errand to Holland; whereupon they debauched him
likewife, and told him, that if he gave us his tools
(as he had promifed to do on our paying for them),
he would throw himfelf out of bread; and that the
univerfity's leafe would not be worth an half-penny
to us, becaufe they were to lead an injunction againft
it. It evidently appeared, he was in concert with
the King's printers, by the people he brought over
with him; one of whom was a fuperanuated failor,
who ingenuoufly confeffed his ignorance; and, after
eight days ftay with us, went home again, although
he was under contract for a year at weekly wages.
Another of them, to excufe his ignorance, told us he
was bred a baker, and had been but two years at the
prefs. The other two were father and fon; the father

was

was a little old man between sixty and seventy years of age, and both so weakly, that they took four pulls at the press instead of two that the English made, who mocking them for their practice in their business, the son, being ashamed, ran away from us in two months. Our new overseer, being along with them at Cambridge, and having no other plates to work upon, but the former uncorrect ones (which he himself had condemned) caused cast off a sheet, which he sent up to London, and which met with approbation; having done his utmost to save his own reputation, and conceal the ignorance of those he had brought from Holland. After this, my partners used their pressing instances to persuade me to go down to Cambridge, which I refused till the contracts should be signed, and the transference made. But telling me, that would take a time, and that the people would be out of work, they gave me an holograph write of John James, signed by him and Fenner, wherein they confirmed to me £ 100 to be paid yearly, or quarterly, for the use of my family; thirty shillings a week for my own subsistance; and likewise obliged themselves to confirm to me one fourth of the profits that should arise from the work, and to extend their obligation in form with all expedition, which, by their verbal promise, was to have been done within six weeks thereafter: having complained of their former payments, they assured me I should be paid punctually for the future. But after seven weeks stay at Cambridge (Fenner having sent down his brother to be cashier), I had no greater payments made me than at the

the rate of ten shillings *per* week: having made
pressing demands in terms of our agreement; this
Fenner told me, that if I were not satisfied with what
he gave, I might go about my business, for they
could do the work without me. By this time having
got a sheet of a Bible made by the direction of this
new overseer, which appeared more beautiful then
any hitherto done, Fenner, hearing me so much com-
mend it, pretended to have a curiosity to look at
it, but lifting it up from the place where it lay to a
better light, dropt it; observing this, I ran to take
up what might be unhurt, but he knocked even
what remained whole to pieces, which shewed 'twas
not an accident, but real design. I soon after difcovered their plot: for, having placed all my tools
and instruments in order at Cambridge, his brother
at London and he thought they could do the business
without me, and so sought all opportunities to fall
out with me; for it was plain from his breaking of
my plates (the goodness of which was owing to our
new overseer's improving of the pages, and pre-
serving of such pages as were sufficient for the work),
that, if they found they could succeed in their design, they would impose upon John James, by making him believe they could perform the work better
than myself, and so have no more occasion for me.
This new overseer staid only ten days at this time that
I was at Cambridge, when the messengers actually
came down with the injunction; who having sent for
him, he kept them company all that night, and
desired them to conceal themselves till he should get

all

all that was due to him (which was only three guineas), and be gone for London, which he accordingly did next morning; and they appeared that afternoon, and laid on their injunction, which in few days after was removed by a decree of the chancery in favour of the univerſity. Our overſeer having now left us, this Fenner our clerk (being a few weeks before an ironmonger) aſſumed the direction as overſeer likewiſe; and made always choice of the worſt plates for the preſs-men to work on, and ſent theſe bad impreſſions to John James, which he ſhewed to ſtationers that he expected would be purchaſers, who attributed the faults of the impreſſion to the badneſs of the paper. Fenner having got already as much from John James as he could expect he would be willing to launch out on this affair; he made a demand of £500. for this paper, which Mr. James refuſed to pay his ſhare of, telling him that he was informed it was nothing but the refuſe and rubbiſh of his ſhop, and that he ought not to have furniſhed paper without the advice and conſent of the concerned, as had been agreed on by our minutes. Then Mr. Fenner applied to Mr. Mount and Mr. Page, who had a conſiderable mortgage on Mr. Baſket's privilege of printing; Mr. Baſket being to receive £11,000. due to him by the Government, with which he deſigned to pay off that mortgage: Fenner hearing of this, conjecturing this a proper time, made propoſals to conjoin Mr. Mount and Mr. Page with him in the univerſity's leaſe, which he had ſtill in his own name. Thereafter he came to Cambridge,

D where

where I acquainted him how haughtily I had been
used by his brother as is above related ; and told
him, I would go to London to see John James, and
provide proper persons to carry on the work, and
have our contracts signed, which ought to have been
done three months before that time.   He told me,
I should get no more papers signed than what were
already, for John James would advance no more
money, and would be no longer concerned ; but that
he had taken care of himself, and was to take-in Mr.
Mount and Mr. Page for sharers.   I then told him,
I had his signed obligation for a fourth share, and
would go to London to let Mr. James know his design, who had already laid out so much money on
that affair.   Finding me obstinate, he begged me to
stay fourteen days, and make the Calendar of a
Prayer-book, that he might have one of them bound
in order to shew it to Mr. James, and that he would
endeavour to get him to continue his concern, and
to bring him to Cambridge in that time ; which they
failing to do, I went to London : but before I set out,
I thought it fit to remove part of my tools, at least
so many of them as should disappoint him, or any
other, in the discovery of any part of my invention.
I likewise carried with me specimens of most of the
sheets cast off, to compare them with what Mr.
James might have got sent him from Fenner.   Mr.
James took out of his pocket those sheets sent him
by Fenner from Cambridge ; amongst which was
one done upon fine paper and sealed, as formerly
spoke of, which he judged to be from the type,
                                                    and

and faid there was no comparifon between it and
the other fpecimens for beauty; and his brother
Thomas James being prefent, and feconding the
fame, the fheet was opened out, and my feal being
found on the middle of it, they were both convinced
that that impreffion was from my plates, and that any
defects they complained of in the others were owing
to the infufficiency of the paper. Next day I went
to call for Fenner, but he would not appear. But
hearing I was come to London, he went down the
day after to Cambridge, where he and his brother
impudently broke open my work-houfe-door, and
finding the material part of my tools gone, applied
to trades-men in the place, thinking to make up what
was wanting; but he could not defcribe, nor they
conceive, what he meant, though he was there fix
weeks about it. When he came back to London,
he perfuaded John James, that, could he have back
my tools, he would make good the undertaking; and
to that end he propofed a meeting with me, to engage
me to go back and replace my tools as they were
before, and I fhould be paid punctually thereafter.
Thefe infinuations fo far prevailed with John James,
that he went into the concert with Fenner againft me,
and gave him fifty guineas as part of his fhare of the
£ 500. for paper above-mentioned : when we met, I
defired to get from Mr. Hamilton the contract in his
hands to be figned; and that Mr. Fenner fhould
transfer the privilege of the univerfity. This
they declined, and faid they would make another
paper equally valid, which John James wrote him-

felf,

felf, and which was a contract for twenty-fix weeks in place of twenty-one years. By this I perceived that their defign was only to get me to carry back my tools, to be more attentive to my performance for difcovery of the myftery, and then to fhuffle me entirely out of the bufinefs.

In the twenty-fix weeks time, they expected I would finifh the half of a Bible, and the half of an Octavo Prayer-book. I told them I faw through their aim, and parted with them. Then Fenner went a fecond time to Cambridge, and practifed for two months with as little fuccefs as before : at his return, he called us to another meeting ; and I carried along with me a country-man of mine, a member of parliament, to whom they offered a fheet of clean paper, to fill up what articles he thought fit for my advantge, if I would return to Cambridge. This gentleman an-fwered, that I had a friend in the place that under-ftood matters of that kind better than he, and de-fired them to appoint an hour and place ; but ac-cidently dropping his name, was known to Mr. Fenner, having heard him plead a caufe in the Ex-chequer in Scotland : when the defendant was feem-ingly to have loft his caufe, this gentleman recovered it to Fenner's great furprize ; which made him believe that gentleman would be too many for him to meet with on my affair. The appointment, however, was made ; but neither he nor James kept it. Some days after, my friend the member of parliament and I met with them in another place, where were the two James's and Fenner. Thomas James, being the

intimate

intimate of Mr. Mount and Mr. Page, was informed
by them, how far Fenner had been bargaining with
them for the privilege of the univerſity; which John
James hearing, told Fenner that he was a knave and
a rogue, and had all along picked his pocket, but
that he would ſtrip him to the ſhirt for his money.
After this, my friend and I gave over hopes of getting
matters accommodated; but he went to my Lord
Iſlay (by whoſe aſſiſtance we had obtained the leaſe,
which was granted ſolely for the encouragement of
my plate-way), to ſolicit his lordſhip to intercede
with the gentlemen of the univerſity for redreſs of
my bad treatment. But this viſit was unluckily
timed; for one Mr. Page an attorney (his lordſhip's
doer at London, and likewiſe for Fenner) being preſent, and hearing application made to his lordſhip
in my behalf, ſaid, I had been ſufficiently rewarded
for what I had done; that I had got £700. of their
money, and that I was old and blind, and that my
partners could perform my undertaking to better pur-
poſe than I could do myſelf. After this, my friend
and I made it our buſineſs to meet with this attorney,
when I had my accompts drawn up, to ſhew him
how far he had been miſinformed. But he would by
no means meet with us, ſaying, Did we imagine to
ſeduce him from his client's intereſt? and that he
would affront my friend, if we gave him any farther
trouble. My friend being obliged to go for Scotland, I never had an opportunity to give my Lord
Iſlay any farther account of my misfortunes. I went
afterwards to Cambridge, to look after my houſehold

3   furniture,

furniture, and the remainder of my tools that I left behind me; but Fenner pretended to detain both furniture and tools for what of the latter I had carried off before, though at the fame time my partners were debtor unto me in £ 240. by their engagements to me, befides my fhare of the plates and profits arifing from them. I could by no means prevail with Fenner to let me have my furniture, tools, or my cabinet where my papers lay. When I came back to London, another friend of mine and I met with Fenner, to whom we propofed to fubmit our difference to the determination of two gentlemen, to be chofen by each of us; to which he anfwered, that he was content, provided I would find bail for what demands he might have on me; to which my friend replied, that I fhould find bail for £ 5000. yea, £ 10,000. if he would do the fame but for £ 2000. But Fenner, hearing this frank offer of my friend and me, declined the fubmiffion; upon which a fubftantial neighbour of his being prefent, told him, that certainly his caufe muft be bad, that he would not truft to the arbitration of two honeft men. Before I left Cambridge laft, I was informed by one of my countrymen who wrought in the houfe, that they had printed off 20,000 copies of a fmall Prayer-book of one line, 10,000 of another Prayer-book of two columns, from my plates made from the fame type; and 10,000 more of an octavo Prayer-book of a larger letter, the one half whereof from plates, and the other from types; befides 10,000 Bibles in manner of this laft mentioned Prayer-book, which

when

when working in the common-way, one third of
thefe types were picked out, Thomas James having
underfized them when he undertook to adjuft them,
though I had all along wrought my plates from thefe
unfized types. After all, I took counfel of Commiffary
Graves at Cambridge, and Mr. Peters counfellor at
London, whom John James had likewife advifed
with; and both agreed that we fhould join in pro-
fecuting Fenner; which Mr. James confented to, but
fhifted me off fo often that I could not wait longer
at London: and thus I was obliged to leave my affair in the fame fituation, and come home to Scotland, without ever having been able ever fince to get
redrefs or fatisfaction for the injuries done me by my
partners.

W. G E D.

II. Supplementary Narrative of GED and his Invention;

Written by his DAUGHTER.

MR. WILLIAM GED, who was a goldfmith in Edinburgh, had been for fome years concerned in paying a relation's printing-houfe fervants, and in his abfence often thought how much money might be faved, and how cheap Bibles and Common-prayer-books might be bought, could a method be fallen upon to make plates for each page; and being affured by a good printer of the advantage that would accrue, he immediately turned all his invention that way, and gave up exceeding good bufinefs, by which he had maintained his family very genteelly, and had faved money. He had alfo improved the Goldfmith bufinefs in many branches, which he liberally communicated to the trade as foon as he made them. But now he turned all his attention to making plates for printing, and threw out much money upon making very expenfive experiments, and feveral years painful and hard labour; and at length obtained it with the cheapeft and eafieft-got materials.

By this time his own ftock was gone. But a friend of his, who had money, and wifhed to ferve both him and himfelf by this improvement, joined him; but neither had knowledge in printing, nor could procure proper work that would do juftice to the performance.

All

All were in arms againſt it ; which induced Mr. Ged to cloſe with Mr. William Fenner, an Engliſhman, who was in Edinburgh at the time. The narrative dictated by himſelf can beſt explain how he was uſed there, and continued till 1733, when he came home, and the bad ſuccefs he had met with ; which proceeded from no failure on his part, but his credulity. His friends, however, were anxious to have a ſpecimen of his performance printed here ; which was at laſt done by ſubſcription. But the difficulty of a compoſitor ſtill remained, and none could be got to do it; his ſon James Ged being then about ten or twelve years old, it was thought proper to breed him a printer ; and he was not much above a year at the buſineſs, when, with the conſent of his maſter, he was allowed to come in the night-time, when all the other compoſitors were gone, and ſet up the forms for his father to caſt off the plates from ; by which means Salluſt was finiſhed 1736. A number of the copies ſtill remain unſold. Mr. William Ged, while at Cambridge, had the fortune to be known to ſome very reſpectful perſons there, who regretted much his uſage, and wanted much to have him replaced printer again, in which Mr. Robert Smith chancellor, and the biſhop of St. Aſaph, were very powerful agents; which encouraged Mr. Ged and a gentleman of property (who was to join him in carrying on the printing) to go to Cambridge 1742. But it happened ſo unlucky, that the univerſity had juſt before that provided themſelves in a great quantity of new types, which they wiſhed to make experiment of at that

E   time.

time. His son James Ged, wearied with many dif-
appointments, went off in 1745, was apprehended
in Carlifle, and condemned with colonel Townley;
but, through Dr. Robert Smith's intereft with the
duke of Newcaftle (upon his father's account) and
fome others, was reprieved; and after being liberate
1748, there were gentlemen under contract with
Mr. William Ged to have him come up to London,
as his fon James was a fufficient printer; which he was
upon the eve of doing, and had all his utenfils new
fit up, and fent for Leith to be fhipped of, when he
fickened, and died October 19, 1749. Thus ended a
very laborious, innocent life, and he had fortitude to
bear himfelf up amidft his many fevere trials and dif-
appointments with chearfulnefs. I muft not omit
one proof he gave of the love of his country, and his
difdain of enriching himfelf at his country's expence.
He had offers from Holland, repeatedly, either to go
over there, or fell them his invention; but he
would not liften, as he faid he meant to ferve his
own country, and not to hurt it, as it muft have
done, enabling them to underfell by that advantage.
After Mr. Ged died, his fon James Ged got up all
his tools to London, and the gentlemen engaged
would have carried on bufinefs with him; but he
had not fo much of his father's genius as his younger
brother William Ged, who, being likewife tired with
repeated difappointment in his father's invention,
though he had the genius for it, left the place, and
went to Jamaica, where he did well and was much
efteemed; and as foon as he had made fome hundred
pounds,

pounds, remitted the money to his brother James at London, to buy a font of types, and bring over all his father's utenfils with him, as he knew he could perform it; unluckily Mr. James left the tools to be fhipped by a friend of his, who moft ungeneroufly kept them to make trial of his fkill himfelf in that way, and the tools were never heard of more; which was no fmall difappointment to William, and what he regretted to his laft hour, 1767. His brother James died the year after he left England.

III. An Account of some of the Advantages of that
Improvement in the Art of Printing, invented
by William Ged, late Goldsmith in Edinburgh;
with Proposals of a Subscription for enabling
his Son, James Ged, Printer, and now the only
Possessor of this Valuable Secret, to carry it into
farther Ex cution, for the Public, and the Benefit
of his Family. Dated London, May 29, 1751.

R*Eceived of*   *the*
  Sum of   *to be deposited in the Hands*
of   *, for a Fund to enable me to carry*
on my Art of Printing by Plates; *which Sum I oblige myself to repay*
out of the Profits of my Work.

THE nature of this Improvement in the Art of
Printing being so little known, it is thought
proper to give the following short account of it:

As to the Invention itself, it consists simply in this;
That Mr. Ged, from any types, of Greek or Roman,
or any other character, forms a plate for every page,
or sheet of a book, from which he prints, instead of
using a type from every letter, as is done in the common way.

The improvement upon the Art, by this curious
invention, is principally considerable in relation to the
Three most important articles of Printing, viz. The
Expence, Correctness, and *Beauty and Uniformity of the
letter.*

1st, The

1ft, The faving on types appears remarkably, no more being neceffary for making plates for any book than what are requifite for compofing only one fheet. When the firft half fheet is compofed, Mr. Ged makes his plates for it while the fecond half fheet is compofing: The types of the firft half fheet are then taken down and made ufe of for the third, whilft plates are made for the fecond, and fo on till the book be finifhed; with much lefs interruption than in the common way of printing, in which the compefitors are frequently ftopped for want of types, till large impreffions of a former fheet are thrown off: but Mr. Ged's method is not liable to this interruption, he being able to make plates for one half fheet in lefs than two hours, which affords an immediate return of types to the compofitors.

In making plates, the types being neither ftrained by a prefs, nor clogged with ink, as in printing from them, are not in danger of being broke, nor do they fuftain any preffure that can wear them; by this means the charge of types, which ufed to be fo great, becomes next to nothing, from the fmall quantity required, and the lafting of fuch as are neceffary.

The expence in printing will be much diminifhed by faving on the article of paper. In the common way, there muft be fome hundreds and frequently thoufands of copies of a book thrown off at firft, to anfwer the common charge of the prefs, which, if the book be long in felling, occafions a confiderable lofs from the intereft of money given out for paper and prefs-mens wages: whereas, in this method by plates,

2   · 100,

100, 50, 20, or any number of copies may be thrown off, according to the brifknefs or flownefs of the fale.

Upon thefe accounts the charge of a book, which bears but one edition, may be more eafily defrayed than in the common way of Printing; but in books that run through many, and in all ftandard and claffical books, for which this improvement is chiefly intended, how obvious and confiderable is the advantage! For, after the common charges are defrayed, by printing off confiderably fewer copies than is generally done in the firft edition of books, every copy afterwards caft off will not amount to the twentieth part of the charge of a copy in the fecond and fubfequent editions reprinted in the common way ; all the expence of compofing, correcting, and new types, being by this method entirely faved, together with the intereft upon paper and prefs-mens wages as aforefaid.

2dly, Books printed in this way muft more infallibly be correct ; for where an error happens, and errors will fometimes efcape the moft exact corrector, they can eafily be amended upon the firft difcovery. Words, and even fentences (provided they can be contained in the fame bounds with thofe to be taken out) can be corrected without deftroying the plate ; at the worft, the charge of plates for a few pages is very inconfiderable: and when a book is once correct, which from this facility it is natural to expect it foon may be, it remains fo for ever; whereas in the common way of printing there is as great, or perhaps greater, hazard of *errata* in the fecond and following editions as in the firft.

3dly, Mr.

3*dly*, Mr. Ged, by repeated experiments, has fhewn to conviction, that there is no diftinguifhing the print from his plates from that of the types from whence thefe plates were formed: fo that it is plain, the print by his plates muft be as beautiful as Field's, Bleau's, Elzivir's, or any of the moft celebrated printers, provided the types from which the plates are made be equally good with theirs. And here it is natural to obferve, the very beft types will always fall reafonably to be ufed, fo few being neceffary; the letter will be beautiful and uniform through the whole book, as clear in the laft page as in the firft, every plate having only its own work. This is not the cafe in printing with types, which are employed fheet after fheet till they are worn out, and occafions that inequality of beauty which fo often appears in the end of books of great length.

Mr. Ged, the inventor of this ingenious and ufeful improvement, by an unwearied application for many years, in which he had occafion to make trial of an almoft infinite variety of experiments, at laft brought it to perfection: but, by a fatality not uncommon to men of merit and ingenuity, he never reaped the fruits of his own induftry. After ftruggling many years with great difficulties, always baffled in his expectations by fome misfortune or other, he died about a year ago amidft a deferving family, in very indifferent circumftances, by his large expences in the unfuccefsful profecution of his difcovery, and fuch as has put it out of his fon's power to carry it on without affiftance.

By

By the help of this fon, whom he bred a printer, and to whom alone he taught his art, Mr. Ged compleated plates for a Salluſt, which he actually printed, at Edinburgh, in the year 1736; and though the badneſs of the types (the only types he could then obtain) from which theſe plates were formed, made it impoſſible for him to make the impreſſion remarkably beautiful; yet the many copies of it in the hands of the curious ſerve at leaſt as a convincing and indiſputable proof of the reality of the improvement in general. It is hoped, that the world will no longer allow this deſerving family to languiſh in obſcurity while one of them is poſſeſſed of a ſecret ſo apparently uſeful, and which, in the event of his death, would be loſt for ever to the publick.

It is humbly propoſed, That gentlemen, lovers of learning, and encouragers of ingenuity, will have the goodneſs to open a ſubſcription, to enable James Ged, the ſon of the inventor, to proſecute his father's art. He has all the tools, but much ſpoiled by diſuſe; moſt of them need to be repaired, and many to be entirely renewed: but for this, and all other expences neceſſary for carrying on the work, it is propoſed, the ſubſcribers ſhould agree upon ſome perſon to receive and have charge of the money ſubſcribed, which ſhall not be laid out but with his knowledge and approbation: and Mr. Ged will give all the ſecurity in his power that the gentlemen ſubſcribers ſhall be gradually reimburſed out of the profits of his work, in ſuch proportions as they ſhall think proper.

IV.

IV. Mr. Mores's Narrative of Block-Printing.

From his Dissertation on Founders.

THE method of Block-printing, firſt practiſed by the Chineſe and Japoneſe, and purſued in the firſt eſſays of Fauſt, the European inventor of the preſent art, before the more excellent method of printing by ſeparate types had been deviſed by him and Schoeffer, was performed by engraving the matter upon blocks of wood, every block containing a page of the work which was to be printed; and in this manner was printed the *Speculum Morientium*, and other maculatures of the art.

About the year 1730 *, one Fenner took it into his head to revive this ancient method, but with improvement: inſtead of planks and engraving, he uſed caſting and plates of metal. Thus; the matter was firſt compoſed in the uſual way: then the form was affuſed with ſome ſort of Gypſum, which, after it was indurated, became a complication of matrices for caſting the whole page in a ſingle piece.

* Ged's plan was firſt put in execution in 1725; his connexion with Fenner commenced in 1729, and it continued till 1733. N.

F   The

The project required money, which Fenner wanted : fo Mr. John James (the brother of Mr. Thomas James) then an architect at Greenwich *, was taken into the fcheme, and aftewards Mr. Thomas James himfelf ; and the partnerfhip at length confifted of

Mr. John James,

Mr. Thomas James,

The faid Fenner, and

James Gadd [Ged] ;

the laft of whom was in the rebellion of 1745, a captain in Perth's regiment, was arraigned of high treafon, pleaded guilty, and begged to be recommended to mercy : and his life was fpared on account of his knowledge in this method of printing which was thought to be ufeful †.

In the purfuit Mr. Thomas James expended a confiderable part of his fortune, and fuffered in his proper bufinefs ‡ : for the printers would not employ

---

* John James was confiderably employed in the works at Greenwich, where he fettled. He built the church there, and the houfe of Sir Gregory Page at Black-heath, the idea of which was taken from Houghton. James likewife built the church of St. George, Hanover Square, the body of the church at Twickenham, and that of St. Luke, Middlefex, which has a flanted obelifk for its fteeple. He tranflated from the French fome books on Gardening. See Walpole, Anecdotes of Painting, vol. IV. p. 48.

† See his Sifter's Narrative, p. 26.

‡ " His death," fays Mr. Mores, " which happened in " the year 1738, was accelerated by an unlucky attach-" ment to a method of printing long fince rejected, and at " variance with the improvements of latter times."

him

him becaufe the Block-printing, had it fucceeded, would have been prejudicial to theirs.

But the hiftory of their progrefs is briefly comprehended in two letters which are owing to this publication;

" Reverend Sir,

" I am adding One to the number of typographical hiftorians : but my fubject is a branch only of that hiftory which has not been treated on profeffedly before.

" In the profecution of it I have occafion to fpeak of the method of Block-printing : or that of printing by caft plates inftead of fingle types, a method which received greater encouragement at Cambridge, than it hath been honoured with in any other place.

" I have now before me a printed addrefs to The Univerfity, figned John James and Company, humbly fuing for the privilege of printing Bibles and Common-prayer-books by this method. The addrefs has no other date than this chronological circumftance to afcertain its time, that it was made about three years after The Univerfity had granted their (then) laft leafe to The Company of Stationers, which I conjecture was about the year 1736, and I apprehend that The Univerfity condefcended to their requeft : for I remember to have been told fome years ago by a ftraggling workman who had wrought there, that both Bibles and Common-prayer-books had been printed, but that the compofitors when they cor-

rected

rected one fault (which was only to be done by per-
foration) made purpofely half a dozen more, and the
prefs-men when the mafters were abfent battered
the letter in aid of the compofitors: in confequence
of which bafe proceedings, the books were fuppreffed
by authority, and condemned to *et piper & quicquid*,
&c. and that all the chandleries in Cambridge were
full of James's Bibles, and that the plates were fent
to the King's printing-houfe, and from thence to
Mr. Caflon's founding-houfe to be melted; an in-
fpector ftanding at the furnace to fee the order fully
executed."

" This, Sir, is all that I have heard of the matter;
and if any thing is untrue or defective, be fo kind as
to correct or add.

" What I particularly defire to know is,

1. Whether Mr. John James was the firft who en-
gaged in this attempt; or whether * * * * * [*this
query was founded on a miftake: a fuppofition that Mr.
John James here mentioned was Mr. John James the
Letter-Founder. He was not; he was the Uncle of our
Founder.*]

2. Who was the inventor: for the invention (if a
revival may be called an invention) was not their
own.

3. The method by which they caft fuch large
plates and fmall letter fo truly, if the fame be not yet
a fecret.

4. The dates neceffary to render the foregoing account more complete.

5. Whether

5. Whether they printed any thing befides Bibles and Common-prayer-books; for I have the plate from which the enclofed page of Salluft * was printed: it was given me by a gentleman of Cambridge, who cannot recollect how he came by it; it feems to have received a ftroke from the wrong end of the ball-ftocks, and to confirm the teftimony of the ftraggler." * * * * *

In anfwer to which thus writes *The Reverend Dr. Richardfon, Mafter of Emanuel,* and with a precifion which we have not met with before : for the fcience of typography, although formerly exercifed by fcholars, and now certainly is an appendage of a fcholar, is but little underftood by thofe who ufe it.

" The firft application which was made to the Univerfity by James and Company for printing Bibles and Common-prayer-books by blocks inftead of fingle types was early in the year 1730, for I find that a fyndicate was appointed to treat with him 6 June in that year; who, being ftrangers to the bufinefs of printing, made fo favourable a reprefentation to the fenate, that a leafe was fealed to him 23 April, 1731. In their attempt to fucceed, the partners funk a pretty large fum of money; but I do not find

* Mr. Mores, when he wrote this letter, was not aware, that the whole volume of Salluft had been printed from blocks. The page which Mr. M. has exhibited as a fpecimen had been greatly injured before it came into his poffeffion.   N.

that

that they completed any one book * by *block*. One, I think, was carried on for some time, but finished by types at laft. After fruitlefs attempts for three or four years, the thing was given up, and application was made to The Univerfity for a frefh leafe to print Bibles, &c. in the common-way, 23 Sept. 1735; and this was refufed.—I do not find what rent was paid. If any, it was very confiderable : for when I was in office in the year 1738, finding a large arrear due, by ufing fome threatning expreffions I recovered £50. took up the old leafe, and fo had done with them.

" One Fenner was the principal perfon concerned, and the projector of the fcheme : James was an architect, and lived at Greenwich, and was taken into partnerfhip as having money. Fenner died infolvent in or before the year 1735, for it was his widow † who applied for a new leafe in that year.

" Thefe

* By Ged's Narrative (fee p. 12.) it appears that they had *finifhed* two Prayer-books.   N.

† Mrs. Fenner was afterwards married to Mr. Waugh, an apothecary, whom fhe furvived.   At a fale of her effects in 1768, I purchafed a quantity of wafte metal which had been many years accumulating; among this parcel was a great variety of metal blocks.   One of thefe (a hand-bill for Dr. Stoughton's Cordial Elixir) I have preferved : and have alfo by me an accidental curiofity; a fmall lump dug out of the ruins occafioned by the conflagration in White Fryars, Jan. 30, 1712-13 ; which, by having been
compreffed

" Thefe Sir, are all the particulars which I can recollect relating to this affair." * * * * *

In refpect to the defign itfelf, we may obferve that the fears of the printers were groundlefs, and the villainy of the workmen fupererogatory : for had the enterprize at firft fucceeded, it muft foon have funk under its own burthen : the difficulty of botching an error which having efcaped the eye of the moft vigilant corrector might cafually be ftumbled upon by an abecedarian; the great weight of metal and dead money ; the capacity of ftowage for that metal ; the care which muft be taken in repofiting the plates, as an ill-fated ftroke would fpoil a whole page ; the more than ordinary wear of the exterior letters of the form, which would fpoil a whole page likewife ; the conclufive bomb-dab of a finifhed prefsman at the end of his beat, fo notorioufly deftructive to a ftanding job, would all contribute to render a defign abortive which hath only this advantage to boaft, that a man may be a printer without a fingle letter in his houfe. Add to this, that the *caft* being three defcents removed from its parent the fharpnefs of the letter is obtunded, and the beauty of the prototype is vanifhed away.

Ged, after he had obtained his pardon, followed his bufinefs for fome time as a journeyman with Mr.

compreffed between two folid fubftances, exhibits on its oppofite fides what Mr. Mores would have called, an impreffion *en creux* and *en relief.* See Diff. on Founders, p. 67. N.

Bettenham :

Bettenham: afterwards he commenced mafter for himfelf at a houfe in Denmark-court in the Strand; unfuccefsful there, he privately fhipped off himfelf and his materials for the other fide of the Atlantic; and, whether it were that having efcaped the one fatality he met with the other we know not * ; but nothing hath fince been heard of him. ·E. R. M.

* Mr. Mores was but little acquainted with the perfonal hiftory and misfortunes of James Ged. He went to Jamaica, where his younger brother was fettled as a reputable printer, and died foon after his arrival at that ifland. See p. 26. N.

₊ In the Running-titles of pages 29, 30, and 32, read " JAMES GED's Narrative."

F I N I S.